Huff

the grumbling pigeon

First published 1976

Childerset Pty Ltd
601 Little Bourke Street, Melbourne, Australia

ISBN 0 909404 02 X

Printed in Hong Kong

Huff

the grumbling pigeon

Story by
Esta de Fossard

Photography by
Haworth Bartram

CHILDERSET

Huff was a pigeon.
He lived in a pigeon house with his
mother and father and sister.

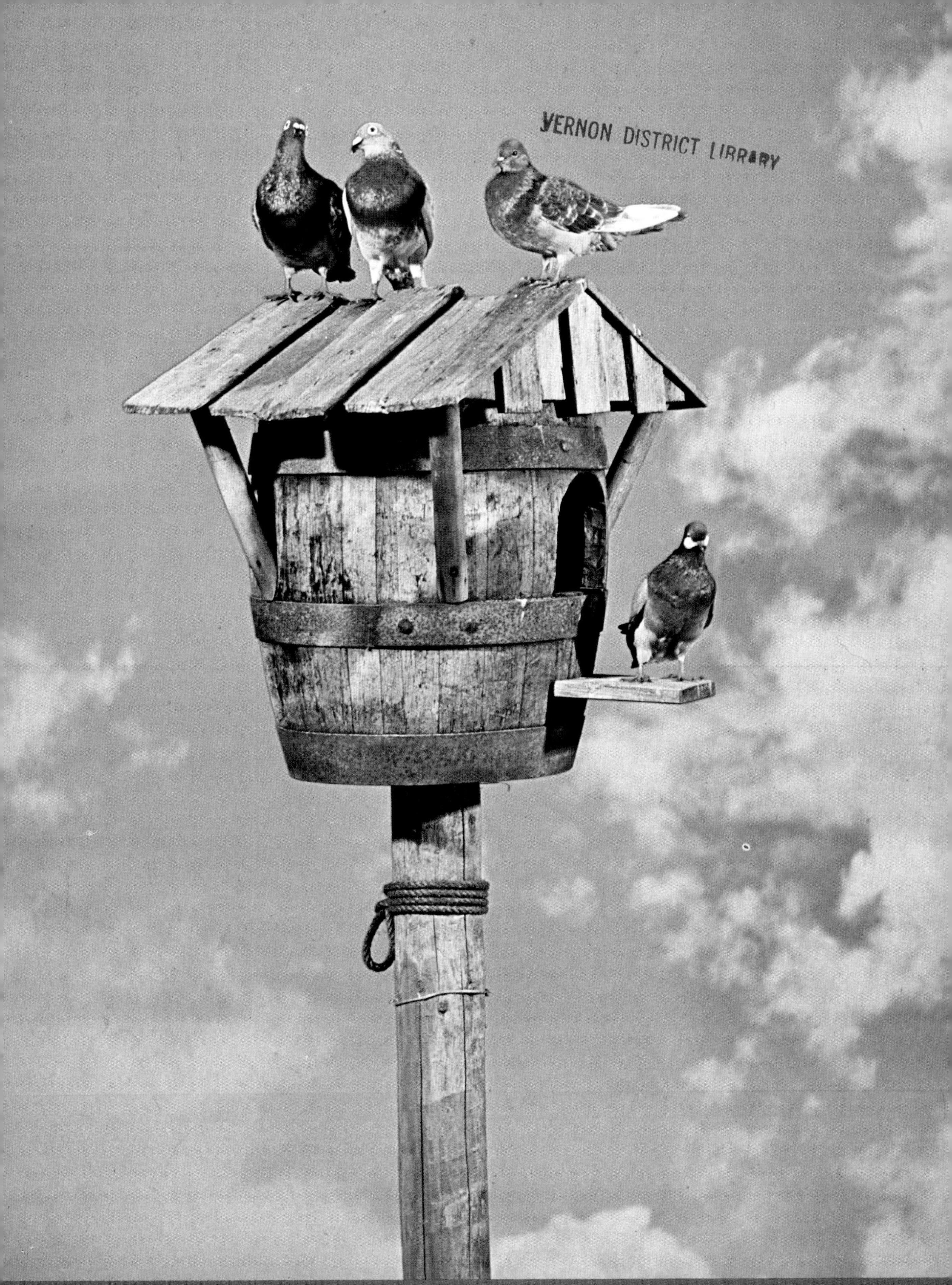

Huff was a grumbler. He was like one
of those silly people who pout and pull ugly
faces when they can't have what they want.

He was always complaining.

He grumbled that his perch in the
pigeon house was not as comfortable as
the perch his sister had.

When he saw the next-door cat staring up at the pigeon house he was sure she wanted to eat him first.

He complained that his sister always ate more than he did.

Nothing suited him.

He had nothing to do.

He was always bored and miserable.

Then a great day arrived.

Huff's father looked at his two children and
said "Today I'm going to teach you to fly."
Huff's sister was very excited. She ruffled her
feathers and flapped her wings. "Oh, let me
go first," she said. "I'm sure I can fly easily."

But Huff sat on his perch and grumbled.
'I'm not going to fly. It's far too hard."
'No, it's not" said his father. "Look!"
And he took off from the edge of the pigeon
house and flew into the air.

It looked so easy. And he looked so graceful.

But Huff stayed on his perch.
"It's too windy" he said.

Then it was time for Huff's sister to try.
She flapped her wings and took off.

She was a bit shaky at first, but soon she
was flying in graceful circles around the garden.
"Oh, come on, Huff" she called. "It's great fun."
But Huff refused to move. "How can I?" he said.
"There isn't room."

So every day Huff sat and watched his sister fly
round and round the garden.

One day his father said, "Well, Huff, if you won't fly, you'll just have to stay here by yourself. We are all going off to the city for the day."

So Huff watched miserably while his whole family flew away and left him alone.

He had nothing to do.

He looked down at the lawn and saw the cat playing. He looked at the tree and saw the sparrows flying around.

Then he looked at the house where the people lived and saw something strange.

Smoke was coming from one of the windows.
The house was on fire!

Huff thought the people would soon come out of
the house to stop the fire, but no-one came.
He was very scared. The house would burn down
and there would be no-one to feed him.

Huff thought the fire might spread. It could
reach across to the pigeon house and then Huff
would be burned too.

He looked around in terror, wondering what to do.
But all the time he knew what he had to do.
He had to fly. He had to fly down to the house
and warn the people.

The ground was a very, very long way down,
but the fire was coming closer.

"Why did this have to happen to me?" Huff
grumbled. But he spread his wings. They
felt strong. Perhaps he could fly after all.
If only he had listened to his father's lessons.

Now he would have to trust to luck.

He flapped his wings once or twice—and jumped.
Then he was flying! It was easy. Huff
could not imagine why he had been so scared
before. He almost forgot about the fire.
But suddenly he was right in among the flames.
He was frightened, but he knew he had to keep going.
He had to reach the house and warn the people.
He flew through the smoke and found a window.

Huff tapped on it with his beak. No one came.
So he knocked again, and kept on knocking as hard
as he could. But no one heard him.

What could he do?

Then Huff remembered what his father had told the family about fire.

He flew away from the heat and smoke, over the trees until he could see a bright red alarm on the side of a building.

He struck the glass with his beak until it broke and pressed the alarm.

BREAK THE GLASS & PRESS THE BUTTON

FIRE
ALARM

Everything seemed to happen at once.
A big door flew open, firemen slid down a pole
and climbed on to fire engines, and three fire
engines raced out of the fire station.

Huff flew back to the house.

The fire engines raced down the drive, firemen climbed down quickly, hoses were pulled out, and water was sprayed everywhere.

And the fire was put out.

When his family came home Huff was sitting on a branch of a tree. His father was very proud when he heard what Huff had done.

And Huff was proud too.

He flew round and round the garden. "Flying is fun!" he shouted.

From then on Huff was very busy flying around and doing interesting things.

And he was never bored or miserable again.